Samuel French Acting Ed

Blackberry Winter

by Steve Yockey

|| SAMUEL FRENCH ||

ISBN 978-0-573-70849-7

www.ConcordTheatricals.com
www.ConcordTheatricals.co.uk

FOR PRODUCTION ENQUIRIES

UNITED STATES AND CANADA
Info@ConcordTheatricals.com
1-866-979-0447

UNITED KINGDOM AND EUROPE
Licensing@ConcordTheatricals.co.uk
020-7054-7200

Each title is subject to availability from Concord Theatricals, depending upon country of performance. Please be aware that *BLACKBERRY WINTER* may not be licensed by Concord Theatricals in your territory. Professional and amateur producers should contact the nearest Concord Theatricals office or licensing partner to verify availability.

MUSIC USE NOTE

IMPORTANT BILLING AND CREDIT REQUIREMENTS

BLACKBERRY WINTER was originally commissioned and developed by Out of Hand Theater. The company presented a workshop production in Atlanta, Georgia from April 15-19, 2014. It was directed by Adam Fristoe. The cast was as follows:

VIVIENNE AVERY . . . . Carolyn Cook
WHITE EGRET . . . . .Maia Knispel
GRAY MOLE. . . . . Joe Sykes

BLACKBERRY WINTER was first produced on September 16, 2015 at Salt Lake Acting Company in Salt Lake City, UT (Cynthia Fleming, Executive Artistic Director). The performance was directed by Sandra Shotwell with sets by Keven Myhre, costumes by K.L. Alberts, lights by James M. Craig, composition and sound by Jennifer Jackson, and puppet design by S. Glenn Brown and Linda L. Brown. The production stage manager was Jennie Sant. The cast was as follows:

VIVIENNE AVERY . . . . April Fossen
WHITE EGRET . . . . Kalika Rose
GRAY MOLE. . . . . S.A. Rogers
PUPPETEERS . . . . Mary Helen Pitman, Connor Nelis Johnson

BLACKBERRY WINTER additionally opened across the 2015-2016 season as a National New Play Network rolling world premiere at the following: Actor's Express and Out of Hand Theater (Atlanta, GA), Capital Stage (Sacramento, CA), New Repertory Theatre (Watertown, MA), Oregon Contemporary Theatre (Eugene, OR), Kitchen Dog Theater (Dallas, TX), and Forum Theatre (Silver Spring, MD).

CHARACTERS

VIVIENNE AVERY – A woman, forties, an exercise in poise that may be a bit frayed at the edges, but she's fighting to keep everything "just so." Her hair is perfect, her skirt is perfect, her silk blouse looks expensive, but her pumps look comfortable. Her humor is a bit dark, her sarcasm a charming defense mechanism. She may have a light Southern accent. Years of success, meticulous planning, and an eye for detail have in no way prepared her for this.

WHITE EGRET – A bird, a woman, she's sharp, observant, social, full of herself, a real problem solver. White balloons tied to one hand keep it aloft & otherwise useless, a pair of thick glasses, ballet shoes, some sort of diaphanous shirt or wrap open over a tank top & leggings, or at least something to achieve the idea of being elongated and above it all. She has pretty clear opinions on the Gray Mole.

GRAY MOLE – A mole, a man, he's blind, a bit cranky, used to feeling his way, and would rather dig than anything, including interact with the other animals. He's blindfolded with white muslin, hands tied together in the front with thick rope, a gray t-shirt, maybe a hoodie, jeans, socks with heavy boots that may be untied, something that feels a bit misanthropic and grounded. He's not a fan of the White Egret.

The actors playing the **WHITE EGRET** *and the* **GRAY MOLE** *should be visible during the play. They should not operate any puppetry themselves unless they can remain in sight. The physical descriptions here are meant to represent characteristics or qualities. As long as the spirit is observed they should be whatever works best with given performers.*

AUTHOR'S NOTES

The playing space is relatively bare with a large scrim for shadow puppetry and a stool or seat on either side. Objects on some sort of pedestals, differing in height, are scattered around:

> A white business envelope (sealed with a letter inside)
> A letter opener
> A pile of silk scarves
> A small box full of recipe cards
> A red pen
> A tiny wooden horse
> A small dropper bottle of Iodine
> A pair of scissors
> A piggy bank of some kind
> A bottle of hand lotion
> A small iron

A gardening trowel
A bundle of white balloons & a pair of thick glasses
A length of thick rope & a strip of white muslin
A wooden box full of photos

In the North American south & midwest, "**Blackberry winter**" is a colloquial expression referring to an unexpected cold snap that often occurs in late spring when the blackberries are in bloom.

The origin myth is illustrated through **shadow puppetry (or video)** on a large scale. During the presentation, the Gray Mole and the White Egret share Vivienne's wry humor and a loose, free quality. The cosmogonies feel brighter, but are not "precious."

The two animals may be on stage throughout or may come and go during the cosmogonies, so long as their final exit is definitive.

Inspired by pastoral ideals of simplicity, nature, and community, the Gray Mole and the White Egret "speak" in **villanelles** largely composed of pyrrhic tetrameter.

There are "scene breaks" through the script, but ideally the performance will flow through as one undertaking.

1. Envelope

(Pedestals holding objects fill the space, different heights, some clustered, some alone. Nothing cluttered though, everything has a clean feel and seems to be exactly where it should be. Only one pedestal stands empty. It need not be obtrusive, but it is alone in having no object. There is a single chair, simple & sleek.)

*(**VIVIENNE** enters carrying a white envelope. She's wearing a silk scarf of some kind.)*

(She drops her purse next to the pedestal with the scarves, places a hand on her hip, and exhales deeply as she shakes the envelope. It feels like she might even have a personal grudge against this particular envelope. She crosses to the empty pedestal and slaps the envelope down.)

(She begins to walk away, but stops to take in the audience. She glances back at the envelope and gives a knowing smile...)

VIVIENNE. You see I know what's in that envelope. It's a letter. It's a very formal looking letter from my mom's assisted living facility. My mom is suffering from, no, no, my mom is "living with" Alzheimer's disease. And the related dementia. And it's getting worse. Of course it's getting worse, that's a stupid thing to say, that's all it can do.

Hello.

And I strongly suspect that envelope is the official notice that the well-meaning people at her assisted living facility think it's time for her to move on. To a nursing home. Which is quite simply outside my sphere of understanding at this moment.

Hello, again. In case you can't tell, I find the very idea of that envelope annoying. No, antagonizing. That's what it is.

Someone, let me just, someone sat in their cookie cutter office with plush carpet that's a little worse for wear and printed out that letter, signed it, maybe they signed it, maybe it's all digital there, and then they folded it up. Someone licked that envelope and probably didn't even give it a second thought. Why would they? They don't know it's horrific.

Oh, and the letter is going to "feel" like it's full of compassion and regret. That sentiment will be entirely undermined by the little number at the bottom unintentionally reminding me it's attached to an account. This is the form letter that's sent when they feel, institutionally, that it's time for your loved one to move on to the next "step on their journey towards peace." And that sounds like a commercial for euthanasia, so you'll forgive me if I'm not ready to "be understanding" yet.

So we are leaving the envelope over there. I say, "we are" leaving it over there, I really mean I am. We just met so please don't feel like you need to be complicit in my impending nervous breakdown.

My mom.

My mom, Rosemary Davis, a truly beautiful woman, has been dealing with this for three years now. Well, we got the diagnosis three years ago, before that who knows. Three years, getting worse. Those are important bits of information. And sometimes I'm a terrible person. That's another bit of important information you should have, I suppose. And I should say: I don't know what you thought we were talking about, but this is the thrust of it. So if you signed up for something else, feel free to go. I won't be offended. Or more accurately you won't be able to tell that I'm offended because this smile...

(She smiles.)

Is made of granite.

Ah, I also make really exceptional brown sugar apple pies, coconut cakes, several different breads, and divinity. People actually pay me for my baked goods; it's not an empty boast. That's another thing to know. Wonderful desserts and a bullet proof smile. Maybe that will make up a bit for the terrible person thing in the end.

Out of necessity, during this time of crisis, I've become a really "proactive family care manager." That's my adopted title that I tag onto the end of other big, life-defining nomenclature: "Vivienne Avery: wife, mother, daughter, small business owner, and proactive family care manager."

The title sounds like I'm taking the reigns, asserting coordination of Mom's care. Which is true. But it actually means I'm piecing together a plan of attack. No. No, that sounds like there's a chance of victory, don't think of it like that. There has to be a better way of describing it.

I suppose I'm piecing together a coherent, well-executed surrender. A way of waving the white flag that ensures Mom is comfortable. God, that sounds, that's not what I'm doing either. Unfortunately, the "proactive family care manager" in me is feeling a bit reactive and is in no way prepared for that letter.

(She gets up, grabs her purse, pulls out a compact, and checks herself, paying particular attention to her hair.)

I don't drink but lately I've become jealous of people who do. And I'm intensely aware of how that sounds.

End 1. Envelope

2. Bottle of Lotion

(Once satisfied, she puts it away, replaces the purse, crosses to the lotion and begins rubbing some into her hands.)

(She takes a deep breath and tries to perk up.)

VIVIENNE. You should see the place, the assisted living facility. It looks like a really nice Residence Inn. Not a middle of the road affair, but one of those deluxe Residence Inns that you stumble upon every once in a while and think, "I really lucked out." A place with real plants. Not silk plants, but real, healthy, well-tended plants. And hot coffee. And side tables with magazines in perfect rows. You can just feel the hospitality painted over everything. In fact, I've taken to just calling it the "Residence Inn."

Mom picked it out. She's always had very specific tastes. She would always say, "Now honey, I know what I want and I'm not afraid to make that clear to people. How else will they know?" And Jesus she is not bashful. She took two steps into the Residence Inn and said, "This is the place." She deserves nice. It is very nice. Everything just so. Little luxuries.

But sometimes I think, "Who's that for?" It's appealing, aesthetically, but what's that in the end? Don't get me wrong, I want Mom somewhere nice, clean, safe. She can't be at my house for so many reasons, not the least of which is her own safely. And the fact that she simply does not want to be there, which I have to respect. Well, I do not "have" to respect it, but because of the safety concerns I pretend to respect it. So I'm saying it's nice that it looks like a Residence Inn, but does that really matter if there's no individualized care? Like that letter, it only "feels" personal.

Individualized. Personal.

Individualized. Personal.

These are words that I find myself saying a lot. They have to know her. I'm absolutely sure, regardless of her mobility or the outbursts or, they just, they would not have sent that letter if they really knew her. I'd rather the whole building look drab on the outside and then be personalized down to the smallest inch for her on the inside, just for her.

Well not drab, but I'd take cotton over silk, ordinary over fancy. I'd rather drive up to a completely unremarkable building and have someone waiting outside who knows my mom, really knows her. Someone who says, "We know you love to bake, Rosemary. And we really need your help to shape these loaves. Can you help us do that?"

Clearly she doesn't need to be anywhere near a working oven now, but I know that just shaping the loaves would trigger something, a memory, a sense of usefulness or purpose. I spoke to an administrator about that idea. He listened, patiently, as I explained my thought process, all of the reading I've been doing. He promised me he'd figure something out.

They're letting her fold the napkins in the dining area. It's a start.

I don't mean to make it sound like they don't care. Or I do mean to make it sound that way, but only because that envelope is really pissing me off. They do care; I have to remind myself they do care. They must. They do. And listen, I'm probably sounding like someone who knows what's "good." I do not know what's good for her. It isn't even a question of what's good or bad in dealing with this fucking awful disease, I shouldn't swear, with this awful disease.

> *(She goes to her purse, pulls out her wallet, finds a quarter, scans the room for the piggy bank, and drops the quarter in.)*

I use my son's old piggy bank as a swear jar. It's for the entire family. But if we're being totally candid, I use it the most. So like I was saying, it's not a question of what's "good."

Individualized. Personal.

Individualized. Personal.

(She picks up the envelope and begins scanning for the pedestal with the letter opener. She spots it and heads over.)

Important words to keep in mind when orchestrating all of this. Because somebody has to be in charge of the sinking ship. And the ship is sinking.

(She picks up the letter opener.)

But…sometimes if you don't actually open the envelope with bad news then all of the bad things inside don't exist yet, right? I sound ridiculous. Maybe it's just a bill. I'd take an unexpected and catastrophically high bill over what I suspect is in here. Because if I'm right then it means a whole new chapter of change. Of aggressive change.

(She sets down the opener and returns the envelope to its pedestal.)

End 2. Bottle of Lotion

3. Recipe Box

*(She looks at her wristwatch and taps at it in
disbelief.)*

VIVIENNE. This isn't exactly how I imagined my day
unfolding. But my day never really unfolds as planned
anymore. Oh God, just hit me in the head with a
hammer, I sound so full of angst. I'm not. I'm really not.

*(She locates the small plastic box full of
recipe cards and retrieves it. She opens it and
thumbs through the cards.)*

I run a business out of my home. It didn't start out
that way, or it was never something that I aspired to
do. I just really love baking. The precision in it. The
way good preparation and carefully measured, carefully
observed steps can transform these disparate things
into something beautiful and delicious. My mom was a
baker, I mentioned that? Well, she was an educational
administrator who loved to bake, so the kitchen was
always so warm and full of potential. Watching her over
the pale yellow tiled counter with morning sunlight
spilling in on her hands as they worked. Oh, and the
aromas all through the house.

Hmm. I'm being fanciful. A bit of that is all right
though, I suppose. Lord knows we could all use a bit
of fanciful. I shouldn't speak for all of us; I could use a
little bit of fanciful.

Most days now I have orders from local restaurants,
sometimes events. So I have to start early. Or bake at
night, which can be a fantastic cover for nerve-riddled
insomnia. Although Jack, my husband Jack, my lovely
husband Jack, is definitely getting wise to me. He
doesn't say anything, but sometimes he'll appear from
the bedroom in the middle of the night, barely awake,
and give me this look.

(She pulls out a well-worn recipe card.)

There's a gourmet coffee shop where they charge you wouldn't believe how much for a slice of my coconut cake. Which is validating. Now this is important: Some people will look at you with a straight face and say they do not enjoy coconut cake. Those people are ignorant. Not stupid, "ignorant" as in lacking in information.

This is my mom's recipe, here on this card. And any given night now for me goes something like this...

> *(She quickly ticks off the ingredients on the card.)*

3/4 pound (3 sticks) unsalted butter, at room temperature

2 cups sugar

5 extra-large eggs, at room temperature

1 1/2 teaspoons pure vanilla extract

1 1/2 teaspoons pure almond extract

3 cups all-purpose flour

1 teaspoon baking powder

1/2 teaspoon baking soda

1/2 teaspoon kosher salt

1 cup milk

4 ounces sweetened shredded coconut

Also extra butter for greasing the pans and extra flour for dusting the pans. I use three cake pans; it's a personal preference. My mom uses two and God help me I never hear the end of it. Ever. Can I just, if I laid out all of the ingredients and utensils, stood her in this kitchen right now and said, "Mom, make a coconut cake." She would stare at everything, look around nervously, and then come up with an excuse for why it isn't good time right now to bake a cake. Because she doesn't remember. But sit her down to watch me do it and she absolutely knows what I'm doing wrong and has strong opinions about it. And that is "fascinating."

Regardless of her objections, I use three pans. Three gives you thinner layers, but still moist. And I take advantage of the extra surface area later for plenty of icing.

Preheat the oven to 350 degrees and grease your three round 9-inch cake pans and dust them lightly with flour. Then get out the electric mixer...oh, unless you don't have an electric mixer and then good luck to you but I certainly don't envy your lot in life or particularly understand you. We are not the same, as people.

Use the paddle attachment on the mixer to cream the butter and sugar on medium-high speed for maybe 3 to 5 minutes, just until it's light yellow and fluffy. Crack the eggs into a small bowl and I try my very best not to remember all the times Mom let me do this part when I was little because she doesn't remember that anymore and it defeats the purpose of this whole fucking endeavor. With the mixer on medium speed, add the eggs, one at a time. Fuck.

(She continues to move through this while heading to her purse, finding two more quarters, and placing them in the piggy bank.)

Add the vanilla and almond extracts and mix well. A word of caution, what you have now probably won't look pretty. Don't think about that, if you can help it.

Don't think about anything.

Don't think about her screaming about imaginary intruders.

Don't think about the terrible things she said, she doesn't mean them.

Don't think about how sometimes she doesn't recognize you at all.

Don't think about anything.

In a separate bowl, sift the flour, baking powder, baking soda and salt. Set that mixer-that-you-really-should-have on a low speed, alternate adding the dry ingredients and milk to the batter. And you'll find the rhythm of it, the hum, is comforting. This is where it's less precise but you get a feel for it. Or you don't and you're just bad at baking.

Then fold in the four ounces of coconut with a rubber spatula. I use a rubber spatula; you can use whatever you'd like.

Pour the batter evenly into the three pans and smooth the top with a knife. Bake in the center of the oven for 30 or 35 minutes, just until the tops are browned. Now it's probably around 3 a.m. This is the difficult part, the actual baking. It's usually when I make the icing so I don't have any down time for my mind to wander. And the icing is its own adventure, but I'll spare you. You're welcome.

(She puts the card back in the box.)

Practically done. Cool the cakes on your baking rack, spread the icing between each layer, stack, frost the top and sides, and finished. Oh, pat some Angel flake coconut all over the icing while it is still tacky because it makes the cake look like what it's supposed to be. And concrete results matter. They have to matter.

As I mentioned, this is my mom's recipe. She taught me the recipe so it's hers. I suppose if my son, Aaron, ever suddenly wanted to know how to make a coconut cake, he'd think of it as my recipe. But that's never, ever going to happen. He can make eggs and bacon. Maybe a grilled cheese. I'm not going to call it a great shame on the family or anything, but his culinary skills are not impressive.

God willing, he won't have to wrestle with any of this "proactive family care manager" business until he's much older. Or maybe he'll be spared completely. Huh, spared. Spared.

I wonder sometimes, when I'm particularly willing to feel sorry for myself, why some people get to experience this without all of the hurdles, the memory loss and dementia? Of course the physical failing happens to everyone, but Jack's father passed at ninety-one and not thirty minutes before he was smiling, talking to his friends, still all there. He had ninety-one years of being present. He had that. So why this morass for my mom? Which is an insanely torturous question with no good answer, because there are no good answers. But I ask it. Again and again.

(She smiles.)

I want to say that I'm aware all of this is habit. I recognize it as habit and perhaps a kind of social camouflage. And a need to be busy and probably distracted and aren't I just so amazingly self-aware and isn't that lovely?

End 3. Recipe Box

4. Cosmogony:
The Gray Mole and the White Egret

*(She closes the recipe box and puts it back in
its place on the pedestal.)*

VIVIENNE. Okay. So when I'm not baking at night, I find
that I very obviously need to keep my mind occupied
with something. Primarily because if I don't then wave
after wave of anxiety comes crashing in and my hands
start to involuntarily clinch up and I absolutely do not
have the time or space for that, not in the least. Who
does?

So I thought to myself, what might I work on in this
noisy corner of my brain to keep the wolves at bay?
And then I had an idea: I'll craft a story, for myself,
I'll make up a kind of creation myth that explains
why this horrible disease exists. There are stories to
explain death, disasters, aging, plagues, where all of
this came from, I've read them all by now, so why not
Alzheimer's? Of course, this kind of "cosmogony," this
kind of cosmogonical undertaking, is no easy affair.
Because the story should be somewhat comforting and
there's precious little comfort in any of this. And the
story should be elucidating and as far as I can tell none
of the doctors or staff at the Residence Inn can offer
much in that arena to my satisfaction. And the story
should not break your heart.

But no one said it would be easy and it is, after all, a
task meant to occupy my mind. Ah, here we go...

(A man who will play the **GRAY MOLE** *enters.
She crosses over towards him and on her way
she grabs the length of rope and the strip of
cloth. When she gets to him, she ties the cloth
around his eyes like a blindfold and then
begins binding his wrists, hands palm to
palm, in front of him.)*

Now this might look a little odd at first. It's to help with the illusion. I have to sort of use what's handy. It's a fable, sort of, with props. But with this right now, I'm trying to capture an anthropomorphic quality, or the opposite of that, you'll see when it gets started. Just don't be nervous about the blindfold and ropes. All right, there we go.

(She lifts up his blindfold a bit so that it rests on his forehead.)

Is that all right?

GRAY MOLE. Yep.

(He crosses to the stool next to the scrim and perches. A woman who will play the **WHITE EGRET** *enters.)*

VIVIENNE. Great. So you just hold on a second. Now it's your turn.

(She crosses over to the **WHITE EGRET**, *finding and collecting the bundle of white balloons and the thick glasses along the way. She takes the hand of the* **WHITE EGRET** *and begins to tie the entire bundle of balloons around her wrist.)*

This one is a little more obviously whimsical. I'm less worried about how it comes across.

(She places a thick pair of glasses on the **WHITE EGRET** *actress.)*

Is that all right?

WHITE EGRET. It's fine.

VIVIENNE. Excellent.

(The **WHITE EGRET** *crosses to a stool next to the scrim and perches.)*

So this is my first stab at an origin myth. And I'll remind you that I'm a mom, a baker, and a defacto "proactive family care manager." Not a writer. So please hold your criticism. This is the first part, sort of an introduction.

And some of it's in verse. Oh, and the entire thing takes place in a lush, verdant forest. So...

> *(She snaps her fingers and the entire space changes. Suddenly the only light is streaming shafts that appear to flow down through tree branches with hints of green. A warm glow rises to envelop the scrim. An initial burst of forest noises settles into a gentle underscore, a soft suggestion of woodland life.* **VIVIENNE** *watches.)*

> *(Images of a the forest and animals flood the shadow puppetry screen, telling the story. It is almost magic.)*

GRAY MOLE. Once there was a Gray Mole.

> *(The* **GRAY MOLE** *actor identifies himself on the scrim.)*

He had tiny eyes, not very good at seeing, and tiny ears, not very good at hearing. But his excellent nose and his little claws were all he needed to idle away his time digging. Now some animals found the Gray Mole to be standoffish or even prickly.

> *(The other animals move away from him. Maybe they have an attitude about it. He digs into the ground and begins to burrow.)*

But really he was affable enough. He just did much better on his own, away from the hustle and bustle of the forest. He would say:

> *(The* **GRAY MOLE** *actor pulls his blindfold down and transforms.)*

"I'm a gray mole and I can't see
And I dig deep in the dark soil
It's so lovely when I burrow
Rolling thick dirt under old trees
Fully at peace with my mute toil
I'm a gray mole and I can't see

Also my ears are not friendly
To the big sounds above the roil
It's so lovely when I burrow
It can frustrate and just vex me
When the others say that I spoil
I'm a gray mole and I can't see
To be quite fair things get messy
Though it's never my plan to foil
It's so lovely when I burrow
Easier then to just scrape free
Where the thick mud knows I'm loyal
I'm a gray mole and I can't see
It's so lovely when I burrow"

> *(The* **GRAY MOLE** *actor lifts his blindfold again.)*

After all, what does a Gray Mole love more than digging beneath the dirt? And so he didn't concern himself with the business of the forest or any business that was not his own.

> *(The images move up to above the ground.)*

WHITE EGRET. In that same forest lived a White Egret.

> *(The* **WHITE EGRET** *actress identifies herself on the scrim.)*

A beautiful White Egret who was ever so social.

> *(The other animals flock over to be near her.)*

In fact, she made it a point to know each and every animal as best she could. And times were good because everyone was enjoying a prosperous spring where even the worst of enemies had found common ground to share and laugh under the immense, old trees.

> *(The* **WHITE EGRET** *moves amongst the animals. She is almost proselytizing to them, or at least that's the feel.)*

She would say:

(The **WHITE EGRET** *actress stretches out and lets her arm with the balloons drift into the air as if she might be lifted off the ground.)*

"Here in the woods with soft sunlight
Wind through branches rustles the leaves
Where the creatures are so happy
Carefree rabbits and larks in flight
Deer run fleet hooved, their white chests heave
Here in the woods with soft sunlight
From the old owls to the wolf's bite
Mingled banter through the air weaves
Where the creatures are so happy
From the field mice to the bear's fright
Or the blind mole who just can't leave
Here in the woods with soft sunlight
Saddened at heart that this may blight
If we forget all we've achieved
And the creatures are so happy
If it could stay like this just right
Prosperous good no one can cleave
Here in the woods with soft sunlight
Where the creatures are so happy"

(The **WHITE EGRET** *actress lowers her arm.)*

The other animals had all been discussing how they could make sure everything stayed this idyllic. Ideas were tossed about, but nothing sounded very promising. The White Egret, sure of herself in most things, decided she would come up with a plan. She needed to find a way to keep all of the memories safe, to stop any of the animals from forgetting.

And just like that, an idea struck her: a simple, lovely idea. She was sure the animals would be so happy as she rushed to tell them all about it.

*(The lights suddenly shift back to normal.
The screen fades and the* **GRAY MOLE** *actor
and* **WHITE EGRET** *actress go still.)*

VIVIENNE. That's the end of the first part of the story. That's
why the lights all changed and the sounds went away.
You probably figured that out. It's pretty, isn't it? I'm
not saying that because I made it up, it just seems like
a very pretty world for escaping. Of course, it's also an
origin myth for Alzheimer's so it won't stay pretty. You
probably figured that out, too.

End 4. Cosmogony

5. Scarves

*(**VIVIENNE** heads over to the pedestal of scarves. She begins to remove her scarf but pauses when the envelope catches her attention again.)*

(She stops what she's doing, crosses over to the pedestal with the red pen, picks it up, and then crosses to the envelope. She writes something on it and holds up the envelope to display her handiwork.)

VIVIENNE. Can you see? I drew a "frowny face" on it. Out of spite. That's the only reason I have that red pen. Defacing things.

(She puts the envelope back down, replaces the red pen on its pedestal, and returns to the pedestal of scarves. She finishes taking off her scarf and folds it to match the others...)

I know it seems childish. It is childish. But it feels good.

(As she places the folded scarf on top of the pile she suddenly stops and takes in the sight.)

Jesus, this is a lot of scarves. I'm just noticing. It's too many scarves. For me, I mean. My mom is a shopper. Always has been. Not one of those crazy order-everything-you-see-on-television shoppers. Ugh, you know, I throw that word around sometimes: "crazy." I shouldn't. If there's one thing having someone with dementia in your life teaches you it's that you shouldn't toss off meaning-laden generalities like "crazy." Not just people with dementia, anyone cognitively different, anyone who thinks differently than you. For instance you might find scarves wonderful, but I don't wear them.

(She stops.)

Well, you just saw me come in with one, but I didn't used to wear scarves. I don't have the patience for it; I can never get them to look the way I imagine they should. Effortless. When I wear scarves they always have this very deliberate feeling. And as far as I know, my mom was never really much of a scarf aficionado either. But she loves to buy them for me.

(She begins folding again.)

And a part of her memory issues, just a little thing, is that she doesn't remember the last time she gave me a scarf. So it's always time for a new one. Always. But I know it makes her happy, so I let her. When we go on these little shopping excursions, if we happen to see some scarves, I will absolutely let her buy me one. Of course, I'm vigilant in my quest to avoid stores that I know have scarves.

Play this game with me; it's fun. Well, it's not fun, but it's eye opening. The next time you go out shopping, try to avoid scarves. You will not be successful because they're everywhere. Once you start paying attention, really paying attention, they're ubiquitous. Why are there scarves everywhere? What is happening to us as a culture that we need this many scarves?

One Sunday we went to an antique store, an antique furniture store, just to walk around, browse, chat, you get the idea. And sure there were some knick knacks here and there and she wanted to buy one for my husband Jack, a little wooden horse.

*(**VIVIENNE** looks around, scanning the pedestals until she finds it. She crosses over and shows everyone the tiny wooden horse.)*

This. When I tell you that Jack couldn't give less of a damn about knick knacks, I hope you'll believe me. If it doesn't involve college football or sports cars, he's really not interested.

(She moves the tiny wooden horse as if it's galloping along.)

But it only cost $10 so I told her, "thank you" because an ingrained politeness, or at least the appearance of politeness, is the one habit I find hardest to break and that was that.

(She sets down the tiny wooden horse and heads back to the scarves.)

Until we got to the back of the store. There was a coat rack, natural enough, covered in scarves. Not display scarves, scarves for sale. In an antique furniture store, because why not? As Mom began to look through them, delighted, my thought process went something like this:

"I really, really hate this antique furniture store."

"Why are there scarves in an antique furniture store?"

"Are they vintage scarves? Could that be the reason?"

"If they're vintage scarves, does that mean they're expensive?"

"Don't let Mom near the expensive scarves!"

But before I could act, Mom had picked out a scarf for me. And she was, of course, adamant about buying it. It was a lovely enough scarf, this scarf, but nothing to write home about. And as I may have mentioned, I need another scarf like I need a hole in the head. Luckily, when something like this happens, I have an easy out. I simply make sure I get the receipt, I take the item back after I drop Mom off at the Residence Inn, and I return it. Then I put the cash back into her account and no harm done. Good plan, right?

(She examines the pedestal covered in scarves.)

Clearly it's not always a success, but despite this pile of evidence to the contrary it works more often than not. But not so fast, for as Mom is having the scarf boxed and wrapped for me, I catch sight of the little hand-written card on the register. And when I say little,

I mean really intentionally, obnoxiously small and unobtrusive:

"No returns. All sales final."

(She picks up one of the scarves.)

This scarf. This scarf right here? $105. What the fuck is it made of?

(She catches herself and as she continues on her rant, she crosses to her purse, yanks out her wallet, pulls out another quarter and puts it in the piggy bank. She then returns to the scarves.)

No, I'm serious. What on earth could this scarf possibly be made of?! It's not silk. It's not. There's no tag, but it's not silk. And listen, I know there are very chic, expensive scarves out there, I'm not ignorant of that. But this is not one of them and unless it's made of spun gold and the tears of butterflies, then I don't think my mom needed to pay $105 for it.

Because. I. Don't. Even. Wear scarves!

(Pause.)

But really, no one can have this many scarves and not wear them. So I do. I do now. And I suppose that means I need to stop thinking of myself as a person who doesn't wear scarves. I'm just...not that person anymore.

End 5. Scarves

6. Iodine

(She stops and looks at the neatly folded pile of scarves. It's almost as if she's created a merchandising display in a store.)

VIVIENNE. What's next, what's next? I should tell you about how we found out. Not "how we found out." I want to tell you about the diagnosis.

*(***VIVIENNE*** holds up a finger for everyone to wait. She heads to her purse. Takes out a quarter. Carries it over, shows it to everyone.)*

I'm going to tell you about the fucking awful diagnosis.

(She drops the quarter in the piggy bank.)

You can begin to see this swear jar is really more of a tax on my language than a deterrent at this point. But it feels at least like trying to do better. There's something to be said for comforting fictions.

(She scans the room for the Iodine bottle, points at it, and heads over.)

Like Iodine; it's one of my favorites. Ostensibly for cuts and scrapes, right? Just a drop or two does the trick.

My sister Marie is two years younger. We grew up in a new construction neighborhood and loved to play in nearby houses that were still being built. Much to my mom's chagrin and against her express commands. So Iodine came in handy when we'd stumble back to the house injured by rough wood or exposed nails. We had a first aid drawer in every room.

That first drop of dark liquid, landing with a jolt, fizzing on the scrape, coming to life, it was like some secret thing to us. Some magic that Mom kept for just such an occasion. And it really looked like it was doing something. Of course, you grow up and discover, as with much in life, Iodine is mostly an old wives' tale in terms of healing. It would frankly be just as effective to slap crude honey on a wound. Really, just walk out to a beehive hanging from a tree, reach in, and scoop honey on your injury.

But it's one of these persistent things we tell ourselves, something we grow up believing. Here's my bottle. And I'd be willing to bet serious money that my sister has a bottle just like this in her house, too.

Marie held my hand when the doctor told us that he "strongly suspected" Mom was suffering from the early stages of Alzheimer's. I usually only see my sister at holidays or a few times a year we'll try to visit. It's about a seven-hour car ride, which is just long enough to not happen as often as you'd like. As girls we were thick as thieves. As adults we're very different people. She is carefree in a way that I just, not carefree, she moves through life less tethered to things. That's the way I should say it. Jack was at work and Marie just went through a divorce, so it was just the two of us. The Doctor has spoken with Mom privately and she asked him to explain things to us while she went to get a coffee. Now I realize she needed a moment, maybe didn't want us to see...

So just Marie and I to hear the Doctor say he "strongly suspected" Mom was suffering from the early stages of Alzheimer's.

"Strongly suspected."

"Strongly suspected."

Marie took my hand, a small gesture, nothing dramatic, and I thought of the Thanksgiving before when Mom was trying to tell us that one of the younger women in her sewing club was getting married. And for some reason she couldn't get the story out, getting more and more frustrated. After a lot of hemming and hawing she offered up that her friend now had an "engagement man." She couldn't remember the word fiancé. And that made the entire story a herculean effort. "Engagement man." It's an example of a work around. When people forget things but just smooth over them. And Marie was holding my hand and I thought of this story and it suddenly became dozens of instances over the previous years and mysterious little injuries and odd accidents, all of which precipitated this appointment. This appointment that I said to Marie was probably unnecessary. Sometimes people just get forgetful when they're older and let's not make a spectacle of these little incidents or make Mom worry. She seems fine.

And suddenly wasn't I foolish?

And suddenly it wasn't about me at all, so wasn't I selfish?

And suddenly I had no idea what to say, which rarely happens.

And obviously what did this mean for Mom?

Because when you hear someone say "early stages" it carries the palpable implication that there are "late stages" and that phrase, in my opinion, has never conveyed a positive connotation.

"Strongly suspected."

Doesn't that just make you want to punch someone in the face? I mean it, with your fist. I'm not a violent person, I'm not an outwardly violent person, but it's infuriating. What if you fell down the stairs on the way out of here tonight, were in excruciating pain, couldn't even bend your ankle, went to the emergency room, they took x-rays and assessed everything, and then the doctor said: "I strongly suspect you injured your leg." Is that satisfying? In my head I'm thinking "Jesus Christ, you are a terrible doctor, just tell us if she has this thing. Just tell us definitively." And I suppose I started to squeeze Marie's hand too tightly, because she pulled her hand away and shot me a look.

Then she asked, "So you're saying, in your opinion, Mom has this?"

And the Doctor said, "Yes."

Then she asked, "And what does that mean?"

And the Doctor said, "It means a lot of things. We can discuss details you may expect and ways to move forward, we can discuss the specific science. The disease is inexorable, but the way it manifests is not the same from person to person. So it's hard to say." Which sounded incredibly clinical and evasive to me, but has turned out to be true.

Then she asked, "So you don't know what it means?"

I could have taken a bath in Iodine.

As we spoke in more detail, he was shockingly comfortable saying, "I don't know." I'm not naïve, but my expectation when I go to the doctor is that they will know what causes something if not exactly how to fix it. So "I don't know" is an incongruity that I was unprepared for. As well as phrases like, "there's some debate" or "many suspect."

So here's what to glean physically about what is happening in the brain of someone with Alzheimer's: Abeta proteins in the brain, they are in there right now, begin to accumulate and create plaques. Then Tau proteins are attracted "somehow" to the Abetas and they create tangles nearby that, well, they do exactly that. They tangle up the neurons. So it's really a series of plaques and tangles suffocating little parts of your brain.

Isn't that fascinating?

Isn't that exceptionally medical?

He gave us a list of books that might be helpful resources. Marie passed it to me. He gave us a list websites we could research. Marie passed them to me. He gave us a folder of information about counselors we could speak to in the neurology and geriatrics departments. Marie passed them to me. And when I say Marie passed them to me, what I really mean is that the doctor handed them to her because she was sitting closer and I gently took them from her hands while she tried not to fall apart.

Of course she has, by now, fallen apart. And I have too. But we try to fall apart in shifts so the other can help put things back together. And based purely on geography, I have orchestrated most of the care. As things have progressed downhill, I've lashed out about that a few times. And that results in fights. The kind of knock down, drag out phone calls that make you never want to speak to someone again. But we do. And sometimes I apologize. And sometimes I mean it. She's not here, she doesn't know.

Frankly, between us, it's much easier to do it myself. To just do the research, read everything, get the medical advice, and forge ahead without having to explain or consult with anyone else.

And Jack has been amazing. I don't mean to make him sound perfect. Candidly, when I say "amazing" I mean that when he does get frustrated he can usually express it without yelling. Even when I'm yelling. The hardest thing he's ever said was one day when he pulled over the car in the middle of one of my diatribes, turned to me, and said, "Vivienne, your mom is going to die. You have to figure out how to keep living." Cut me to the bone. Also wise advice. I didn't speak to him for two days.

(She lets one drop of Iodine on the back of her hand.)

Oh, driving home from the diagnosis appointment, Marie was in the back seat and Mom was in the passenger seat. She turned on the radio and found a country music station that was playing Lorrie Morgan's "Something in Red." It played for a minute; it's such a depressing song do you know it? It's from the early nineties. She's singing about needing to find different colored dresses for different occasions in her life, all of which revolve around attracting or pleasing her man. It's fine, I suppose, it just really does have this melancholic lament to it. If you don't know it, you'll just have to believe me when I tell you it makes an incredibly awkward post-Alzheimer's-diagnosis car ride soundtrack.

Suddenly, out of nowhere, Mom takes off her sunglasses very deliberately and announces, "Girls. I'm fine. I feel fine. And if I start to not feel fine, we'll figure it out. But for now don't you worry, all right?"

(Pause. She replaces the Iodine bottle.)

I smiled at her and said, "All right, Mom." And I looked into the rear view mirror and Marie was staring back at me. I will never forget the look of suppressed panic in her eyes when she also said, "All right."

(She begins scanning the room and her eyes land on the scissors.)

End 6. Iodine

7. Scissors

(She crosses to the pedestal with the pair of scissors. En route, she's already speaking.)

Now would you like to hear something cute? Of course you would, after that? Of course you would. I give Mom her haircuts now. I'm not skilled, per se, but I do a serviceable job. And sometimes I'll put a barrette in her hair because she hates it but it is just the most adorable thing. But mostly she just lets me decide.

(She picks up the scissors.)

That's a blessing when she lets me decide things. She'll say, "Honey, you're in charge now. Tell me where to sit and I'll sit, tell me what we're doing and we'll do it." And thank God we're in that place. For now. But it's a very odd flip that's happened where I'm now responsible for her. I don't mind it, I truly don't. I'm riddled with anxiety and baking until dawn, but it's my turn and she has been she has been wonderful to me. I want to do as much for her as I can. I want to do more than I can.

There was... There was a time in my early teens when I wasn't very kind to my mom. She didn't know how to talk to me and I didn't want to talk to her. I can't give you a reason. But I was cruel in the way that only young people who've never been hurt can be cruel. Casually cruel. Obviously we moved through that, but I think about those times more and more lately. Missed opportunities.

But it did get better. In fact, I truly enjoyed the period of time in between then and now, when we were grown and responsible for ourselves, when we became good friends. I miss that.

(She puts the scissors down.)

We do the haircuts at my house, out on the back patio, and afterwards Mom always offers to sweep up the hair. And that's the ticket. Because she just keeps sweeping.

And something about the movement, the task itself, she's more relaxed and lucid while she's sweeping. Her humor comes back, that biting humor that I'm on the receiving end more often than I'd like. But I'll take it if it comes with the rest of her.

It's just like the loaves of bread idea, or the folding napkins that ideally would have been shaping loaves of bread. There's something about physical activity that not only engages what's still there inside the person but also leads to feelings of calm and usefulness. It's astounding.

Full disclaimer: I am not an expert. I am however well-versed and have read everything, every single thing under the sun about Alzheimer's and the related dementia, every single thing about different theories on treatment, different histories, every fucking Hallmark laden memoir with an inevitable devastating ending about personal survival and grace in the face of this yawning monster.

(She retrieves a coin from her purse and drops it in the piggy bank.)

My home office has a very small corner devoted to mail and tax information pertaining to my business. The rest of the room exists as a cross between an Alzheimer's reference section and the periodicals archive at the county library.

And in my extensive research, I've come across the most amazing things. You know, there is an entire little town, a little planned community, outside of Amsterdam that is for residents suffering from dementia. And everything in that town is built around two core principals: provide a safe, familiar, humane environment and maximize quality of life by keeping them active, simple as that. If you want to wait at the bus stop for a fictional bus all day, do it. If you want to push a baby doll around in a stroller all day, do it. And they have a baking club. Where ostensibly people can bake. There are no medical treatments, there are pills, but what you essentially have for people dealing with dementia is care giving. That's it. Care giving. Do you want to engage them or do you just want to control them?

Institutionalized. Personal.

Institutionalized. Personal.

There's not a facility like that around here. So it becomes a war of inches within an existing model of treatment. Can she make bread? No, she can fold napkins.

> *(Frustrated, she waves her hand and the lights and sound shift back into the forest look and the warmth of the scrim.)*

End 7. Scissors

8. Cosmogony:
Memory Box

(The **WHITE EGRET** *and the* **GRAY MOLE** *still sit next to the scrim as the world transforms again and the shadow puppets come to life on the screen.)*

(The **WHITE EGRET** *lands on a tree branch overlooking the other animals and speaks.)*

WHITE EGRET. After excitedly calling all of the animals together, the White Egret perched on a branch and proudly presented her wonderful idea. She would collect the memories of the animals, store them away in a box for safekeeping, and bury the box deep in the ground.

(She produces a wooden box, opens it, and places it before the assembled animals.)

The animals loved the idea. Placing their memories in a box to keep them safe made sense. They praised the White Egret for her foresight and wisdom. Really they we're just so happy someone had come up with something.

And she, while quietly preening and cleaning her feathers, accepted the praise. Clearly agreed it was an excellent idea, how could she not?

(She collects memories from animals and places them into the box.)

And so she collected the animals' memories to place them, ever so gently, into a small wooden box. Memories are the tiniest, most fragile of things. But in just a raindrop full, lifetimes are held for the reminiscing.

She would say:

(The **WHITE EGRET** *actress stretches out and lets her arm with the balloons drift into the air.)*

"Memories to box kept locked away
Keep them in place and sure secure
So animals remember well
How frenzied squirrels figured the way
Old injuries with chipmunks to cure
Memories to box kept locked away
All histories held tight night and day
In time preserved and we endure
So animals remember well
How sly foxes learned to slow sway
In harmony with twigs and spurs
Memories to box kept locked away
And let practice your worries allay
In this success you will inure
So animals remember well
Without a doubt please if I may
I'm the white egret, my plan ensures
Memories to box kept locked away
So animals remember well"

> *(She closes up the box and the animals move
> off. She digs a hole and drops the box inside.
> Then she begins to fill in the hole.)*

> *(The* **WHITE EGRET** *actress lowers her arm.)*

And with that, she closed the wooden box up tight.
Then she began to dig a very deep hole to bury the box
deep in the ground. Deep down where no one would
ever happen upon it. No one she could think of at least.

GRAY MOLE. In the meantime, the gray mole had carved
out a little burrow and was slumbering away when
something that sounded a lot like digging began to
rumble through the dirt.

> *(Beneath the hole that the* **WHITE EGRET** *is
> filling in, sits the* **GRAY MOLE**'s *burrow. He
> looks up towards the racket above him.)*

Still groggy and out of sorts from sleep, he would say:

(The **GRAY MOLE** *actor pulls his blindfold down and transforms.)*

"Feel of digging shakes loose the dirt
Stirring efforts open my eyes
Who is coming down to see me?
This guest disturbs a dream of mirth
Sudden uninvited surprise
Feel of digging shakes loose the dirt
This kind of dream I have a dearth
So this interruption's no prize
Who is coming down to see me?
Grit and rock fall onto my hearth
Eyelids heavy, hard to revive
Feel of digging shakes loose the dirt
Scanning the deep down less than alert
Feeling for anything I can surmise
Who is coming down to see me?
Crawl ahead, no longer inert
My favorite task is now reprised
Feel of digging shakes loose the dirt
Who is coming down to see me?"

(The **GRAY MOLE** *begins to dig up towards the buried box.)*

(The **GRAY MOLE** *actor lifts his blindfold again.)*

And so the gray mole began to slowly, leisurely dig in the direction of the disturbance. He was in no hurry. Just curious. Just curious.

(The lights shift back and the sound vanishes again.)

VIVIENNE. And that's the end of part two. It's only three parts, if the verse is getting to you. At the very least it must be a nice respite from my gloom and doom.

Gloom and doom might be a bit much, I suppose it's not all bad.

> (**VIVIENNE** *gets out of her chair and heads over to the pedestal with the iron. She stops on her way...*)

It is all bad. It is. But it doesn't have to be all depressing, does it? It can be other things, too.

End 8. Cosmogony

9. Iron

*(She leaves the iron on the pedestal, but lifts
the plug at the end of the cord.)*

VIVIENNE. It can also be amusing, sometimes, in a way.
Well, the word amusing takes on a new context under
the circumstances.

As I mentioned my mom is dealing with dementia,
well there are over fifty causes of dementia, but she
is specifically dealing with dementia associated with
Alzheimer's. And a part of her dementia involves
confabulation. Confabulation occurs when memories
of events, people, the world around us, are fabricated,
distorted or misinterpreted. Essentially, it's when
memories are just made up.

Now it's not lying. It can feel like lying but you have to
remember it's not lying. There is no conscious will to
deceive. The people confabulating do not realize they
are making things up. They believe all of it.

Here is an example of simple one. A while back, when
things were still...

Well, a while back I bought Mom an electric iron
with an automated shut off. As a safety precaution, it
actually turns itself off if it sits for too long. Ingenious.
Of course I did explain this feature to her when I gave
her the iron. And she smiled. And she nodded.

Now as best I can tell, Mom did happen to turn on
the iron a few weeks back and then wander off to do
something else. And the iron did its job admirably and
shut off. So when my mom returned and found it still
plugged in but cold, she decided the only explanation
is that the building has "weak electricity." Not faulty,
in her estimation, just not turned up high enough,
not strong enough. And now she cannot be disabused
of this notion. Really. It's become a plain truth that
she has shared with me, my sister, my husband, the
administrators at the Residence Inn, and probably

anyone who happens by. I'll remind her about the safety feature and she'll just say, "That's all well and good, but the building's weak electricity is the real culprit." Weak electricity. The very idea of it.

(She releases the end of the plug.)

Oh, and I have to tell you about the laundry thief. These get darker as we go, just a heads up in advance. The services at the Residence Inn include laundry. A staff member comes in on a regular basis, removes dirty laundry from the hamper, then return the folded laundry later. Simple.

But my mom, a woman who double majored in education and linguistics, is fully convinced, hand to God, that someone is sneaking into her room when she's not there and stealing her laundry. At first I tried to convince her it wasn't happening explain the laundry service. Let me just clearly acknowledge that was a poor, poor plan. As far as she's concerned, my mom is at the center of a Nancy Drew mystery unfolding at the Residence Inn right now. And I am going to help her solve it. I'm Nancy Drew.

Because it's so important when addressing someone with dementia that you work within their beliefs, navigate inside their confabulations. You agree with them. It's not easy, but it's important. You do not tell them they're wrong, that only makes them afraid or angry. You accept what they say, you go with the flow, and you perhaps try to steer them away from anything particularly frightening. If you can.

I used to watch my mom do this patiently and masterfully with my grandmother. Ironically, Mom used to tell me with a smirk about how when her mother was suffering from dementia, she would always have to find the stolen purse. Someone was always stealing Grandma's purse. Of course my mom would find her mom's "stolen purse" under the kitchen sink all the time. Grandma would put it there for safety's sake, forget, and then convince herself it was stolen. So now when my mom's things "go missing" it does amuse me to remember that story. Honestly amuse isn't the right word. And it also makes me sad. And yes that's the first time I've mentioned that my mom's mom went through this same thing and yes it's clearly something that exists hereditarily and aren't I staring down the future in all this and I can't. I just fucking cannot.

(She goes to her purse, takes out the wallet, empties all of the change into her hands, and carries it all over to the piggy bank. She slaps all of the coins down on the pedestal and inserts one.)

Because it's not fucking about me.

(She inserts a coin.)

It's not fucking about me.

(She inserts a coin.)

It's not fucking about me.

(She inserts a coin.)

It's. Not. About. Me.

(Quietly.) If this could happen to me in my lifetime, then let me never wish away a single moment of this life.

(She takes a breath.)

One more confabulation. Now she hasn't told me this yet, but she's told other people at her facility and word has come back around to me. She currently believes, along with the weak electricity and the laundry thief, she believes that someone has broken into her room at night and held a pillow over her face. Upon hearing this, the questions start. It's not fair to call them concerns yet, but definitely questions:

"Did someone actually sneak in to try to smother her?" Unlikely.

"Did someone come in to adjust one of her pillows while she was sleeping?" Probably not. No night check-ins on the menu.

"Did a neighbor girl hit her with a pillow at a sleepover when she was little and it's coming back to her now?" Possible.

"Is she lonely and just seeking attention?" God, I hope not.

And in the end, what does the actual answer matter? To her, it's something that has definitely happened. This terrifying thing is true and she now remembers it as truth.

(Quietly, almost to herself...) Isn't that awful? Fuck.

> *(She moves back to the piggy bank and drops in another quarter.)*

End 9. Iron

10. Piggy Bank

*(She moves the loose change on the pedestal
around with her finger.)*

VIVIENNE. All right. All right, there's actually an upside to
my rapidly disintegrating decorum and vocabulary.
Besides mildly entertaining some of you, it also helps
to fill this piggy bank and I need to do that as many
times as possible. For a rainy day. Now it's gauche to
discuss money; I know that. And I have never been a
person to do it, but I also never used to wear scarves
so all kinds of things are changing. And if we're talking
brass tacks, let's talk brass tacks.

The monthly facility bill for the Residence Inn clocks
in at $5,000. That covers housing, food, services, basic
cleaning personal laundry, and a staff check-in every
two hours to make sure you're still breathing, etc.

We opted out of the nighttime check-ins, well, for two
reasons. The first is that she needs an uninterrupted
good night's sleep. The second, now I'm going to say
this and I want you to not react immediately, really try
to hear it. The second reason is that if she were to die in
her sleep that would be a blessing. Clearly it would be
heartbreaking, but compared to the pain and suffering
that some people experience?

When I first said this thought out loud it was what can
only be described as a spontaneous utterance on the
phone with my sister Marie and the minute that it left
my mouth, I expected her to either hang up or begin
yelling. She just sighed and said, "I hope so, Viv."

So it's $5,000 for the Residence Inn. And an additional
$300 for administering her medication and that comes
from the pharmacy at a wholesale price, so it's about
$80. That's not as terrifying as it could be. It would be
more if we added bathing to the tab, which I did one
month in a moment of weakness, exhaustion, I don't
know. Mom received a bath exactly one time from

very patient staff member. And when I say, "received a bath" what you should hear is, "hid in the closet and screamed like she was being attacked." So I give Mom her baths, when we agree that's the thing to do. And I know that will change when we move her to a nursing home. Jesus, I can really only imagine. Because when she screams at me, it's almost like she's...

I will not imagine that.

I will not imagine that.

The good news, the good news is that 85% is covered by Mom's pension from the state university system. Also, Social Security. And my Dad was a Methodist minister, so there's a survivor benefit from the church. We, our family being a collective "we," are in a good position, a deeply lucky position, to be tackling this. For now. But the costs are coming. It's like a fucking avalanche; the further down the hill it gets, the larger it becomes.

>*(She casualty reaches over, scoops up a coin, and drops it in the piggy bank.)*

Investment.

Long-term care insurance is available and at the ready, but we've been saving it for the much higher nursing home costs that are inevitable.

Can I just go back to the bathing thing for a moment? Does it seem like some hugely taxing thing to bathe your parent, a person who spent years bathing you? No, it doesn't. Or even if it does, you deal with it. The cycle of life, we all become toddlers again, however you need to think about it. I was visiting with Mom this morning; we, we're having tea in the little lobby area of the Residence Inn. They make it look like a study. Well, they put books on the shelves. But if you look at them closely, it's easily 70% old romance novels. Which I just love. But I'm having a nice tea with Mom, we're talking about Marie's divorce. But of course she doesn't remember that Marie got a divorce so every time I bring it up it becomes a very fraught conversation.

And on the couch across from us these two people, a man and a woman, easily in their forties, were arguing. And that's being generous because you could palpably feel the aggression between them. These angry whispers like daggers that weren't really even whispers. They were arguing about who would be responsible for bathing Dad because he didn't want to pay for the extra service and she didn't want to pay for the extra service but neither of them wanted to actually do it. Because apparently Dad is a handful and doesn't behave and isn't responding and more and more of this, with the pitch of their voices rising.

I was trying to ignore them, but this is not something I want Mom to have to hear and I definitely caught her eyes darting to the side. No one from the staff was saying anything, so I put on my version of absolute politeness and I leaned over to them, tea still in hand.

"I'm so sorry to interrupt you, but might this be a conversation better served by privacy?"

They looked at me as if I were, in fact, a talking horse.

And now we get to the crux of it. They both had a few choice things to say about minding my own business and how much they paid for these facilities. And suddenly, it was as if I just forgot my context completely. I put down my tea cup, moved to the edge of the cushion, and said:

"It sounds to me like you're in the wrong place. If your father can't be managed during simple tasks like bathing anymore, then you should probably move him to a nursing home and stop bothering everyone here."

   (Pause.)

I said this with no regard for my mom sitting just at the other end of the couch. For the current state of things. The people were taken aback. They got up and walked out. And I wouldn't look at her. I couldn't.

I knew she heard me.

I knew she heard me.

And I thought to myself, please don't let her remember this.

> *(Pause. Her head falls into her hands.*
> *Without looking up, she waves her hand as if*
> *she's waving away the audience. It's a gesture*
> *of "leave me alone." The lights shift into the*
> *forest look and the sounds spill onto the*
> *stage.)*

End 10. Piggy Bank

11. Cosmogony:
Unhappy Accidents

(The **WHITE EGRET** *hops off her perch and steps out.)*

(The forest full of animals appears again on the screen.)

WHITE EGRET. At first everything was as wonderful as predicted and the forest was happy. But slowly things began to change. The animals became clumsy, confused, they began to not recognize each other; they began to forget.

The white egret did not understand how this could be happening. Why was everyone snapping at each other, wandering away alone, sitting quietly without chirping or sniffing or making any other sounds? This should not be happening with all of their memories locked so safely away in a box buried so deep in the ground.

(The animals begin to snap and lunge at each other. Some wander away. The **WHITE EGRET** *flies to a tree branch up above them.)*

It was then that the white egret knew she must check on the box. So she went to the correct spot and began to dig.

(The **WHITE EGRET** *flies over to a specific spot and begins to dig.)*

GRAY MOLE. The gray mole had been ahead of her in digging to the box.

(The images reveal the **GRAY MOLE** *who has tunneled to the box.)*

Only he had come from underneath instead of above. He had no understanding of what the box held, but he felt curious, compelled to get inside and discover its secrets. He would say:

(The **GRAY MOLE** *actor pulls his blindfold down and transforms.)*

"Box of secrets dropped from above,
Deep dark my nose meets wood's hard kiss
With teeth I gnaw again again
Solid and rough, things not to love
Inside my brain I muse what's this?
Box of secrets dropped from above
So I bang bang and knock and shove
I claw through wood my nails amiss
With teeth I gnaw again again

(As the **GRAY MOLE** *gets inside, trippy images colors and symbols of the other animals may flash on the screen or roll by in quick succession.)*

Something inside makes my nose buzz
Something thats taste tongues can't dismiss
Box of secrets dropped from above
Something inside teases my blood
Something so warm and sweet as bliss
With teeth I gnaw again again
Content thanks to contents thereof
I cannot stop, the warmth insists
Box of secrets dropped from above
With teeth I gnaw again again"

(The **GRAY MOLE** *actor lifts his blindfold again.)*

And so he rolled around and gnawed away at the memories inside the box, unaware of what he was actually doing. He ignored everything else, even the sounds and rumbles of digging that inched ever closer.

(The **WHITE EGRET** *reaches the box and pulls open the lid.)*

Until suddenly the box lid was pulled open and he had to squint to see the figure of a large white bird outlined by the sun behind her.

WHITE EGRET. She was horrified by the mole, covered in bits of memory, nesting in the very best reminiscences of her friends, gnawing at their recollections. She let out a shrill call.

> *(One intensely loud, shrill birdcall echoes through the space as the shadow puppet of the* **WHITE EGRET** *looks up and cries out in horror.)*

GRAY MOLE. Terrified, the gray mole scampered deeper into the earth, out of the bird's reach. He dragged as much of the warm, glowing material with him as he could, leaving nothing but the wood from which the box was made. He would go deeper. It would be safer there, safer from the prying eyes and greedy beaks of others.

> *(The* **GRAY MOLE** *descends deeper into the dirt. She flies back to her tree and the other animals stumble around below her.)*

WHITE EGRET. The white egret watched the mole vanish into the dirt and, looking away from the empty box that had been her wise, wonderful idea, took in the forest around her, the forest forgetting itself. She would say:

> *(The* **WHITE EGRET** *actress stretches out and lets her arm with the balloons drift into the air.)*

"Errant digging comes at a cost
Nothing left now save hard splinters
Fading memories lost in the woods
Too much to do to guess what's lost
Lists of musts in gentle whimpers
Errant digging comes at a cost
Inside their minds paths less embossed
All remembrance drifts from center
Fading memories lost in the woods

I could not see from up aloft
The blind gray mole softly enter
Errant digging comes at a cost
No sense of cold, their eyes all glossed
The animals shake and shiver
Fading memories lost in the woods
Outside chilled now, a snap of frost
Some lingering blackberry winter
Errant digging comes at a cost
Fading memories lost in the woods"

(The **WHITE EGRET** *actress lowers her arm.)*

And so, she set about tenderly caring for all of the animals that could no longer fully care for themselves. Helping them as best she could.

(The **WHITE EGRET** *actress removes the balloons from her arm and lets them drift from her hand as her puppet disappears from the screen. She takes off her glasses and sets them on a pedestal.)*

And in a way the forest did remain the quiet, peaceful place she had longed to maintain, save the occasional outburst or noisy confusion. But not in the way she ever would have hoped.

(The **GRAY MOLE** *frees his hands and removes his blindfold as the* **GRAY MOLE** *image disappears from the screen.)*

GRAY MOLE. And the Gray Mole continued to dig. And dig. And dig. And dig. And dig...

(He continues to quietly repeat this phrase as he sets his rope and blindfold on the pedestal. The **GRAY MOLE** *actor takes the* **WHITE EGRET** *actress by the hand, and they leave.)*

(On the screen, the **GRAY MOLE** *continues to dig deeper and deeper. Slowly his path is revealed. It's not just the one tunnel, but*

dozens upon dozens of tunnels intersecting and extending, slowly carving the earth away. Elaborate and devastating. The image fades. The lights return to normal, the scrim goes cold, and the sounds vanish.)

*(**VIVIENNE** sits quietly.)*

(She sits.)

VIVIENNE. That's it. That's the ending I came up with. No reason short of really unfortunate luck. No one's to blame, nothing's fixed in the end, and I suppose she takes care of the other animals forever. And that mole just keeps digging.

(She sits.)

It's not comforting at all, is it?

(She takes a deep breath, gets up, wipes her eyes, and heads over to the pedestal with the trowel. She doesn't have to search for it, she knows exactly where it is.)

End 11. Cosmogony

12. Trowel

*(**VIVIENNE** picks up the trowel.)*

VIVIENNE. I knew right where this was; it's one of the first things I saw when I walked out here. My long dark night of the soul routine is almost over now because this is the bottom. This trowel.

(She examines the gardening tool.)

I use this to hunt for truffles in a family friend's pecan orchards. She doesn't mind; we're not sneaking around under the cover of night or anything. I can use them in my baking, the truffles, sell them at the farmer's market, and it's good exercise for Mom. Or it was when she still helped me. Now she just stands there with this...

(She puts down the trowel like it might be dangerous.)

And they're truffles, so sometimes we find them, sometimes we don't. It's really more about that time together away from the Residence Inn. Away from everything. We'll have our coffee, maybe it's still crisp in the air, maybe it's already warmer. Maybe she'll make a joke at my expense, like I said, but more and more she doesn't say anything. She quietly, slowly shuffles through the pecan trees leaning on her cane not looking at anything in particular.

(She crosses over to a wooden box that is reminiscent of the box from the Cosmogonies. She opens it and a soft glow emerges. She pulls a stack of old photos out. It's a box of memories.)

I'll look at Mom standing in that gentle light coming through the trees and think: Rosemary Davis, you raised me well and I owe you practically everything. A while longer and I'll think: Rosemary Davis, I wish with all my heart that I could take this for you. But a while after that something comes undone. If I look too long, it becomes: Rosemary Davis, who are you? Even now there's so much I don't know about your life and you're disappearing right in front of me. We'll go for walks in the nearby woods afterwards...

> *(She stops herself. Not ready for this story. She holds up a picture of her and her mom. As she continues, she might even carry it around for as many people to see as possible.)*

The problem with looking at someone too long is that you start to see around your idea of that person, you start to see all of the details that compose them; it's why we mostly glance at people. If you look too long even the closest people can start to seem like strangers and that can create a kind of...distance. That's not the right word. Fuck.

> *(She puts the picture back in the box, closes it. She has to put it away in order to continue. She also puts another coin in the piggy bank.)*

Okay, okay...

Okay, like I said, like I started to say, we'll go for walks in the nearby woods afterwards and they're lovely. When it's just the two of us alone in the trees, moving quietly through the trees, and she clearly has no idea where we are and maybe the sun is beginning to set. Everything feels so secretive, so hushed.

And that's when it starts. That's when the reptile part in the very back of my brain rises up; the noisy part that chafes against the base of my skull unless I mute it with cakes and pastries and antiques and well intentioned but horribly depressing animal myths.

"It's never going to get better."

"It's never going to get better."

"It's never going to get better."

"She's never going to get better."

"She's never going to get better."

"There's no one else here."

"She could just get lost."

"She could so easily get lost."

"It would be so much easier for everyone."

"Is it better to just disappear in the woods?"

"Because it's only going to get worse."

"It's only going to get worse."

"It's only going to get worse."

"This is the braver choice."

"This is the braver choice."

"She shouldn't have to suffer."

"She should not have to suffer."

"I don't want her to suffer."

"It's so quiet."

"It's so quiet."

"We're all alone."

"No one would know."

"It's so quiet."

"That rock looks heavy enough to..."

(She covers her mouth as if it wouldn't have stopped on its own.)

Remember when I said that sometimes I'm a terrible person?

(Pause. She finally falls apart.)

None of us can keep from thinking things. Try not to think about something, it's impossible. But sometimes just thinking a thought is enough to see yourself differently. Jesus, even if Mom can't always express herself anymore, she's going to be so unhappy in a nursing home. She won't have her freedom, not in the same way. I understand that's a part of all this, but she won't understand. God help me, she might completely understand and that would be even worse. Oh God. I love her. I love her and want her to be happy. Not happy. Comfortable. And at peace. I don't want it to get any worse. I don't know if I can cope with it if it gets any worse. Jesus, it's not about me!!

(Pause. It takes as long as it takes. She returns to her purse and checks her compact again. It isn't what she wanted to see. She begins to pull herself together as best she can, wiping away tears.)

She doesn't deserve what's happening to her. No one deserves what's happening to her. Earth-shattering observations, I know. She also doesn't deserve to be abandoned in the woods somewhere or something worse by her exhausted, horribly misguided daughter.

End 12. Trowel

13. Envelope

*(She closes her compact and drops it back
into her purse. She smoothes herself out as
best she can.)*

I just need to...

No, I just have to accept that she has the time she
has. That's all. We have that time and we will make it
everything we can. Or I don't have to accept it, but I do
have to get over it. Yes, that's better, because it has to
be about the possibilities. It's about what's still there,
every little thing.

So then I suppose what I'm finally left with in the end
are these two exceptionally large "I can't" ideas that
have to be recognized, that have to be faced. And both
of these radically different ideas must be addressed in
every moment. Ready?

The idea that I can't physically make her brain better.

And the idea that I can't face this.

First: I can't fix her brain. I cannot. That is a fact. I am
powerless. It is a mystery, a terrifying and sad mystery
and there is nothing I can do to make it better. That's
a fact.

Second: I can't face this. That is not a fact. Not at
all. That's a failing in me, a weakness in me. It's
understandable and justifiable, but it's not a fact.
And in that respect I am not powerless. I will not be
powerless. I do not want to be afraid. I do not want to
be the midnight cake baker. And I absolutely will not
be the woman with the rock in the woods.

I have to remember that distinction between Mom
the person, where I should focus, where I have to try,
try, try to live, and "Mom" the problem to be solved,
which involves fixing, which I cannot do. Keeping up
with her health, finding the best care giving, I can do
that, communicating with her, continuing to engage

her, those are the challenges to be faced. She is not the problem.

It has to be about what's left.

It's about what's left.

It's about what's left.

It's about what's left.

> *(She crosses over, grabs the letter opener, and then heads for the envelope. She grabs it up.)*

And this? This is just another step. For both of us. It's just another step towards whatever is coming next. And I can face it. I can do that. I absolutely will.

And all of the fear, well...who has time for that?

> *(She takes a breath, opens the envelope with one swift swipe from the letter opener as the lights quickly swell and then slip away into darkness.)*

End of Play